Oliver McCoy
The Vegetable Boy

Story by Richard B. Joelson

Illustrations by: Annette C. Shumay
Technical Editor: Justen Stryker

Oliver McCoy – The Vegetable Boy
Published by:
SLM Book Publishing LLC
21204 Pontiac Trail #16
South Lyon, Michigan 48178

Oliver McCoy – The Vegetable Boy is a work of fiction. Names, characters, places and incidents either are the product of the author's imagination or are used fictitiously, and any resemblance to any actual persons, living or dead, events, or locales is entirely coincidental. This book was printed in the United States of America.

Library of Congress Control Number: 2011923860
ISBN-13: 978-0-9830039-1-5

Dedication

This book is dedicated to Rosalind, who has been an invaluable resource throughout every aspect of the Oliver McCoy children's book adventure and other writing projects. Eager cheerleader, valuable critic, skilled editor, and wise advisor whose active interest in my creative endeavors has always meant the world to me.

REVIEWS (FROM THE EXPERTS)

Dr. Joelson, we are so thankful that you were able to come in and read your wonderful book to us! We also appreciate you donating a book and giving us bookmarks. Good luck on Oliver's next adventure. MT third grade

Thank you for visiting our class. I learned a lot. I thank you for a lot of stuff like signing bookmarks. You answered a lot of questions. I wish I could be an author when I grow up. EK second grade

Thank you for visiting our class. I love your wonderful book. Thank you for donating your book to us. Sincerely, MA third grade

Thank you so much for coming to our class and reading your awesome book. My favorite part is when you said: when he went north, his friends went south. You are great at writing! EC third grade

Thank you for visiting our class. I loved when you read us your new book and your book that just came out. You inspired me to write my own book. Sincerely, MD third grade

Thank you for coming to our class and reading us Oliver McCoy – The Boy Who Loved Onions and your book coming out soon, Oliver McCoy – The Vegetable Boy. I love my bookmark you signed. When I am older I'm going to consider being an author. From BL third grade

There was a time

when all Oliver ate

Were

NIONS

...and *nothing* else

on his plate

His family REALLY wanted him

to try other stuff

But Ollie said, "I want

for me that's enough"

His mom said…

"Ollie, there are *other* veggies to eat"

Like...

 Tomato

or  Broccoli

or even a  Beet

 9

Maybe an

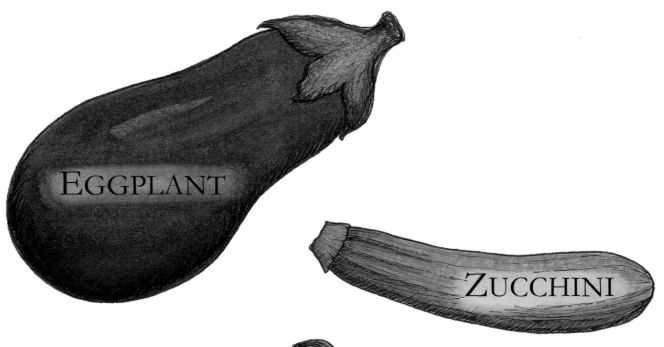

EGGPLANT

ZUCCHINI

PEPPER

11

Or some

PEAS

'Here are some

BRUSSELS
SPROUTS

please try
some of these"

Ollie tried

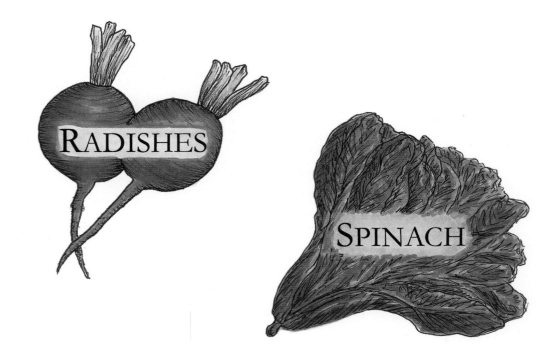

RADISHES

SPINACH

and more

And went with his mom to the…

VEGETABLE STORE

16

They bought…

CUCUMBERS

CELERY

CAULIFLOWER

too

18

SQUASH

and some

LETTUCE

to name only a few

19

He began to like vegetables
and ate them a lot

Especially

POTATOES

when…

Cooked in a

POT

21

He REALLY liked

SPINACH

and to his surprise

He liked it as much as some people like

His dad said, "Hey, Ollie, come follow me

To the backyard,

there's something

I'd like you to see."

Ollie followed him outside and
looked all around…

He looked up
at the sky

And then down
at the ground

27

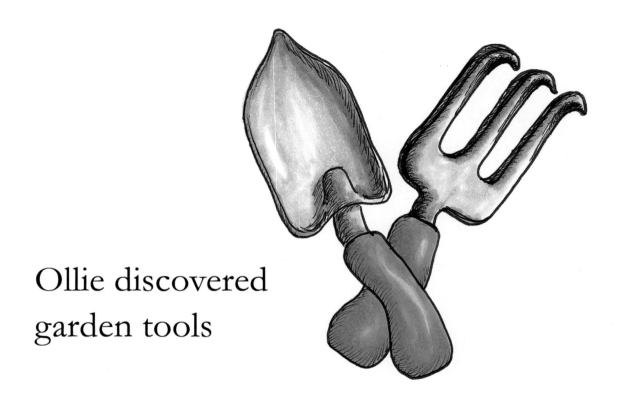

Ollie discovered
garden tools

And some

All of the things that a gardener needs

To make a vegetable garden
of his very own

A place where fresh veggies
can be easily grown

Ollie planted lots of

and

too

31

And

and

GREEN
PEPPERS

LETTUCE

and even a few...

PUMPKINS *and* SQUASH

33

And *juicy*

TOMATOES

34

He even tried

to grow

a few BIG…

POTATOES

36

Before long,

Ollie's garden

gave many a treat

Including

an   ONION

which he *still* loved to eat

While other kids drank

LEMONADE

in a cup with a straw

Ollie said

"I think people might enjoy
veggie juice more."

He gave ALL of his friends
a veggie juice serving

To

MARCY ROY BOB

ANNIE and IRVING

43

Everyone

Ollie's veggie juice treat

Even

JESSICA

JUAN

and his best friend

PETE

45

When people heard about

Ollie's new juice

They said,

WOW!
We'd *like* to try it

And once they drank a

whole

big

cupful

They said, "We think we'd like to buy it."

Ollie said,

I have an idea that's REALLY just grand!

I'm going to open a…

50

"I'll sell my vegetables

and my veggie juice, too"

And

vegetable

SOUP

And

vegetable

STEW

"I'll help

      everyone

           try *new*

                vegetable treats"

Then they can choose

EGGIES

and...

EAT FEWER SWEETS!

THE
END

Until the next Oliver McCoy
       fruit and vegetable adventure…

57